Under and Over

Luana Mitten and Meg Greve

ROURKE PUBLISHING

Vero Beach, Florida 32964

www.rourkepublishing.com

PHOTO CREDITS: © sabrina dei nobili: 3; © fotoVoyager: 4, 5; © Dave Pilkington: 6, 7; © Denis Jr. Tangeny: 8, 9; © Steve Rabin: 10, 11; © Steve Snyder: 12, 13; © Ken Babione: 14, 15; © Carsten Madsen: 16, 17; © Peter Spiro: 18, 19; © Justin Horrocks: 20, 21; © Laura Eisenberg: 22, 23

Editor: Luana Mitten

Cover design by Nicola Stratford, bdpublishing.com

Interior Design by Tara Raymo

Library of Congress Cataloging-in-Publication Data

Mitten, Luana K.
  Under and over : concepts / Luana Mitten and Meg Greve.
      p. cm.
  Includes bibliographical references and index.
  ISBN 978-1-60694-382-3 (alk. paper)
  ISBN 978-1-60694-514-8 (soft cover)
  1. Space perception. I. Greve, Meg. II. Title.
  BF469.M585 2010
  423'.12--dc22
                          2009016024

Printed in the USA

CG/CG

www.rourkepublishing.com - rourke@rourkepublishing.com
Post Office Box 643328 Vero Beach, Florida 32964

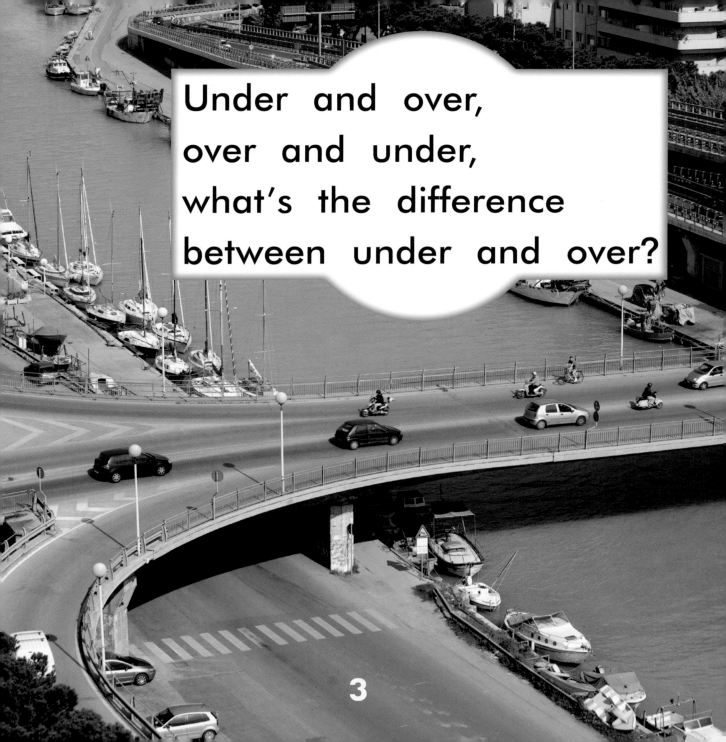

Under and over,
over and under,
what's the difference
between under and over?

3

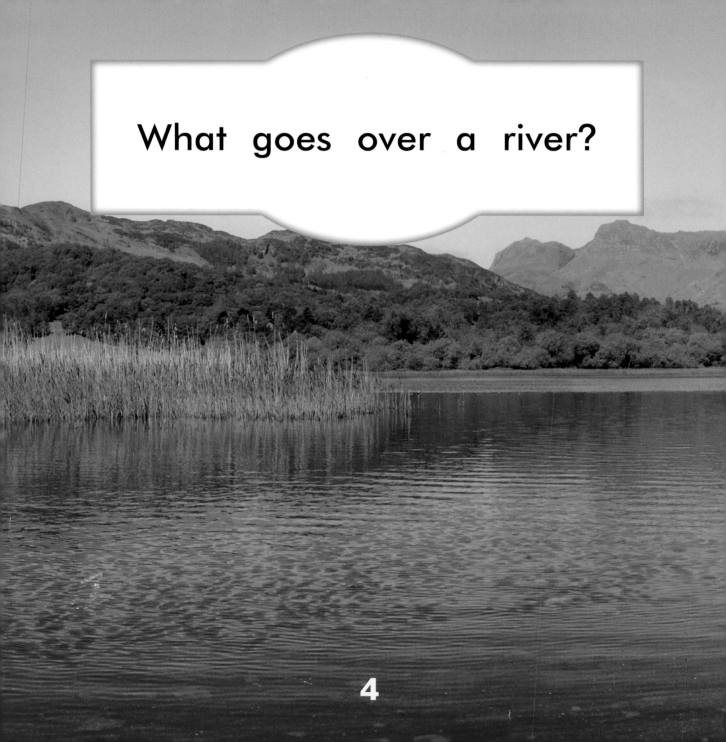

What goes over a river?

5

6

A bridge goes over a river.

7

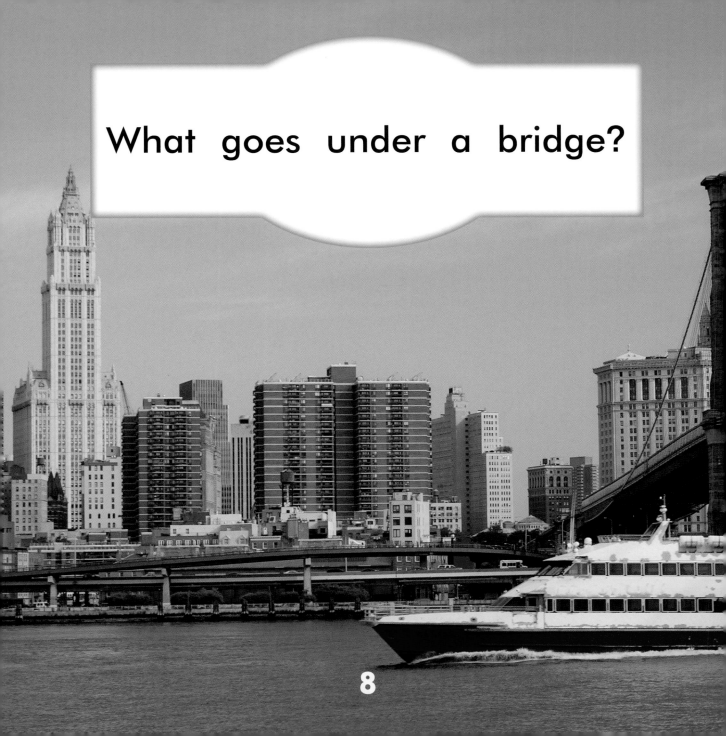

What goes under a bridge?

A boat!
Toot! Toot!

9

10

What goes under a mountain?

A tunnel goes under a mountain.

What goes over a mountain?

14

An airplane!
Wooosh!

16

What goes under a street?

18

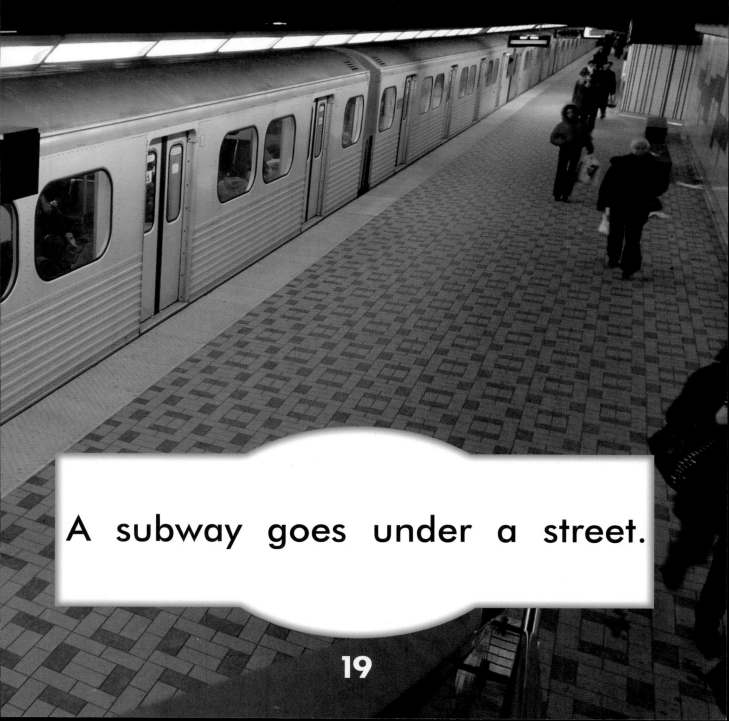

A subway goes under a street.

What goes over a street?

21

22

A train goes over a street.
Whoo! Whoo!

Index

Websites to Visit

members.enchantedlearning.com/themes/transportation.shtml

www.boatsafe.com/kids/navigation.htm

www.dot.state.pa.us/Internet/pdKids.nsf/TrainHomePage?OpenFrameset

About the Author

Thanks to phone calls and e-mails, Meg Greve and Luana Mitten can work together even though they live about 1,200 miles (1,900 kilometers) apart. Meg lives in the big city of Chicago, Illinois and gets to play in the snow with her kids. Luana lives on a golf course in Tampa, Florida and gets freckles on her face from playing at the beach with her son.

Artist: Madison Greve